Contents

Chapter 1

Rosie rarely did as she was told.
And being a not-so-little princess,
she could do whatever she liked
most of the time.

So, when Maidy called upstairs
for the third time, "HURRY AND
GET DRESSED! YOUR NEW FRIEND
WILL BE HERE ANY MINUTE!",
Rosie was still busily sorting out her

clothes in alphabetical order:

B – for BEST DRESSES. Four to be used for parties, visiting royal aunties and uncles and maybe judging dog shows. One made in purple velvet and fringed in ermine, for VERY SPECIAL occasions.

C – for CROWNS. Nine gold everyday ones, and a special one with rubies and diamonds for coronations and visits by other kings and queens.

J – for JEANS. Twelve pairs – one with patches sewn on by Princess Rosie herself.

N – for NIGHTDRESSES. Ten, all white.

T – for TRAINERS. Three pairs. One pair for special, one pair for splashing in muddy puddles, one pair for kicking things and doing other stuff like tripping up little brothers.

Maidy's shout came just as Rosie was about to get to U for UNDERWEAR. She let out a deep sigh. "Not another new friend!" she said.

She turned to Gilbert, her loyal
bear. "Do you remember the last
one, Gilbert? Wilbert Cuthbertson
or Cuthbert Wilbertson – something
like that? He didn't like dolls, he
didn't like skipping, he didn't like
any of the games I wanted to play.

All he wanted to do was try on the suits of armour in the long hall and play war with Daddy's collection of old swords."

Rosie smiled as she thought back. He had challenged the General to a sword fight. The General had drawn his sword and cut off Cuthbert's sticky-up hair with one swipe!

"ROSIE!!!" shouted Maidy, *very* loudly this time. "GET YOUR ROYAL SELF DOWN HERE AT ONCE!"

Rosie knew that Maidy's voice was now too cross to ignore, so she slid down the banister of the very long castle staircase.

Maidy was waiting at the bottom, her arms folded. She pointed to the golden hall and said, "He's already waiting. He might even have got fed up and gone by now!"

Chapter 2

Rosie huffed but decided to do
as Maidy told her. She had just
started along the golden hall, when
something leaped out from behind
the tall dresser and crashed into her,
knocking off her second-favourite
everyday crown!

Before she could get a good
look at it, the thing spoke! Shaking
Rosie's hand hard, it said,
"Hello, jolly old royal person! It
is exceptionally nice to meet you,
old girl! My name is Oliver, but
everyone calls me Ollie. Ha ha!
Snort! Snort!"

And this very strange creature continued to snort and shake the Princess's hand up and down until Rosie was feeling a bit sick.

She scowled. "What do you think you are doing? You can't call me OLD! I am only seven! And I am a princess!"

She carried on, "You are supposed to bow to me, and now you have knocked off my second-favourite everyday crown, and it is probably bent and I'll get into trouble and you are supposed to talk to me like a future queen and—"

"Sorry, old girl!" Ollie interrupted her, grinning wildly. "I didn't mean to upset you. But, anyway, why do you wear a crown all the time? Isn't it uncomfortable? Is it to stop a rhinoceros hurting you if it falls on your head?" And he finished this with another snort.

Rosie didn't answer. She had never met a person quite like this before.

She took a closer look at him. He was very thin, and taller than her, with arms and legs that seemed to get in the way of themselves. His hair was all over the place and he wore big glasses that made his eyes look huge. He was covered in freckles and had a wide, toothy smile. Yes, he did look rather odd.

"Do you always speak in that funny way?" she asked.

"Yes, I'm afraid so, old bean," he said cheerfully. "I was brought up by my uncle, the Old Duke of Frogmorton, and he always speaks like this. The same as everyone did back in the olden days. Can't get out of the habit, don't you know?"

With that, he gave Rosie a
hearty slap on the back. It took the
wind out of her and she staggered
forward.

But she suddenly started smiling.
There was something about this
great clumsy boy that she liked.
Normally the new people sent to be
her friends were quite boring. They
either barely said a word or tried to
show off and impress her.

Ollie seemed like a fun person to be around. Rosie could get up to all sorts of things with him about! An idea began to form in her mind.

"Come on!" she said, grabbing his hand. "Let's raid the cupboards for a picnic!"

Chapter 3

Rosie led Ollie to the kitchens and they crept in as quietly as they could. Cook had his back turned. He was stirring something in a steaming pot, and bits of cabbage were flying about as he chopped and sliced. He was whistling the French national anthem, as usual,

and concentrating so hard he didn't
see them enter. He didn't see them
creep into the larder either.

Rosie gave Ollie a nod and they
each dashed over to a shelf and
grabbed something without looking.
Then they ran away, trying not to
giggle too loudly.

Rosie and Ollie ran as fast
as they could out into the sunny
gardens, Ollie's long legs and arms
flapping around like a scarecrow's.
Rosie led him round the side of the
castle and into the parkland.

They didn't stop until they were deep in the fruit garden amongst the raspberry canes. They flopped down to catch their breath.

Rosie took a proper look at what she had snatched from the larder. It was a big bag of something called "Piggy Scratchings".

"This is not good," she said. "These look disgusting." But she was determined to have her picnic so she carefully tasted one.

"YUCK!" She spat it out. "It's all hairy! No wonder the pigs were scratching!"

Ollie had grabbed a huge bottle of purple stuff. "Mine is called 'Old Moggie's Plum Cordial'!" he said, holding up the bottle to the sun and peering suspiciously at it.

Rosie reached for it, but Ollie shook his head. "Oh no, we can't drink this, old girl," he told her. "I saw Dwayne, our butler's son, drink a big bottle of something that looked just like this stuff and he started talking awfully funny, slept for two days and wasn't at all well when he awoke."

Rosie believed him. She'd seen
what happened to the Admiral when
he drank strange-looking drinks
She poured the Old Moggie's Plum
Cordial onto the raspberry canes.
Then she sighed.

"What shall we do now?" She
looked at Ollie expectantly. "I'm
bored!"

"Mustn't say 'bored', old thing," he said. "It is boring to say 'bored'. There are so many things to do."

"You mustn't keep saying 'old thing', either!" she told him firmly.

But Ollie didn't seem to notice. His eyes grew bigger and more googly behind his glasses and he cried, "I know! Let's have an adventure!"

"How can we do that?" Rosie asked.

"You have to use your imagination!" said Ollie, looking mysterious.

Chapter 4

"Let's pretend we are detectives and solve a crime," said Ollie.

"But that isn't real," replied Rosie. "I want something REAL to happen."

"Wait a minute!" said Ollie, spotting the frown creeping onto the Princess's face. "Do you have any secret rooms in your castle?"

Rosie shook her head, but her eyes lit up. She liked the sound of this!

"ALL castles have secret rooms," Ollie insisted.

Just then, Rosie spotted the Prime Minister zooming by on his tricycle. She sprang up so suddenly from behind the raspberry canes that he jumped and nearly fell off!

"Do we have any secret rooms in the castle, Prime Minister?" she asked.

He regained his balance. "Secret rooms? Hmm . . ." He scratched his head. "I don't think so. But then if it is a secret room, I wouldn't know about it, would I?"

And off he went, looking very pleased with himself.

"He is a funny old chap!" said Ollie in his old-fashioned way.

"But he's right," Rosie said glumly. "If the room's a real secret, how will we ever find it?"

Ollie's never-fading grin spread even wider. "I've got it! Each room in a castle will have a window. So all we need to do is count the windows on the *outside* of the castle and then see if there is the same number of rooms on the *inside*."

Rosie understood. "So, if there is one more window than rooms, then that window will be where the secret room is!"

"That's it! Come on, old thing," he said. "Let's go and look."

Rosie led Ollie to the large green lawn at the back of the castle.

She began to count the windows on the top floor one at a time. "One, two three, four— Argh!" she stamped her foot with impatience. The windows were placed in such a higgledy piggledy way that Rosie had lost count in a moment.

Just then, the King popped his head out from one of the upper bedroom windows. "What are you doing?"

"We are counting windows," Rosie told her father. "To see if there are any extra ones."

"Good. I am glad to see you taking an interest in maths." And he pulled his head inside.

Rosie and Ollie went back to their counting.

"I make it one hundred and twenty-three," she said eventually.

"I make it one hundred and twenty-three, as well," said Ollie.

"Right, let's go inside and see how many rooms there are!"

Chapter 5

They scampered up to the top floor.
The castle was very big so they were
out of breath when they got there.
But they set off again, counting the
rooms this time. It took them a long
time.

"One hundred and twenty-two!"
Rosie called as she reached the hall.

There were one hundred and twenty-three windows, but only one hundred and twenty-two doors. "There *is* a secret room in the castle! But how do we actually find it?"

"Well, next we need to tap all the walls to hear if any of them sound hollow, like a room is behind there!" explained Ollie, who seemed to know lots about finding secret rooms.

"This is exciting!" Rosie shouted.

Prince Billy suddenly appeared. He had followed them around the castle and now wanted to join in.

"Can I help?" he asked. He looked curiously at Ollie. "Is he your boyfriend?"

"No, he isn't! And buzz off!" Rosie said rather grumpily.

"He isn't a bee so he can't buzz off," Ollie told her. "Anyway, he seems like a nice little chap."

Billy beamed. Rosie looked at him, thinking. She had never thought of him as "nice". *You don't know him*, she thought to herself.

But she was having such a great time with Ollie that even her annoying little brother couldn't spoil things.

"OK, you can help," she agreed.

Rosie and Ollie went round the castle, tapping. Prince Billy joined in too, copying them. He didn't really know what he was doing or why he was doing it, but he'd been allowed to join in and had a happy smile on his face.

All the courtiers and ladies in waiting and staff were very surprised at their strange behaviour, but thought it best to leave them to it.

Finally, Rosie, Ollie and Billy went into Rosie's bedroom. They began to tap on her walls, looking for a sign that might mean a secret room was on the other side.

Ollie suddenly stopped his tapping. He pointed to a little hole in the wallpaper that he had made.

"Look at this, Rosie! This looks
like a place where a door knob used
to be. Let's get the knob from your
door and try it."

Rosie ran to unscrew the big brass
door knob from the bedroom door.

Ollie fixed it into the hole in the
wall. "Well, old girl, this is looking
promising. There's definitely a door
under here. But we still need to open
it somehow."

Rosie stared at Ollie in astonishment. There it was: a real door, to a real room. She moved forward and turned the handle. But nothing happened. It was stuck!

Ollie stepped forward to help her, and with them both turning and pulling on the door knob together, it came open with a sudden dusty *whoosh!*

"Let's go!" Rosie whispered dramatically. And they stepped inside, with the little prince at their heels.

Chapter 6

They all coughed as a funny smell of old musty things that had been hidden away for years came out from the secret room.

Cobwebs covered everything, and Billy shuddered. "I hope there aren't any giant spiders hiding in this room!"

It was too gloomy to see if this was true.

Rosie stumbled her way over to the window, which was very dirty on the inside. She used her hand to wipe it clean, and light flooded in.

She gasped as the inside of
the room was revealed. There was
everything she could possibly want
for a day playing with her new friend!

There were lots of different toys,
like dolls houses,

and an old rocking horse covered in
dust with a bird's nest on its saddle.

There were boxes of old, painted
lead soldiers,

jigsaw puzzles and wooden blocks.

Shelves were lined with story books.

The King and Queen had heard the noise of the door bursting open and came running along the corridor. Spotting the hole in the Princess's bedroom, they entered, ready to shriek with horror. But when the King saw what was inside, a huge smile spread across his face.

He held up an old tin box and brushed the dust off its lid. "This must be the storeroom where all my old toys were kept! So *this* is where my toy soldiers went!"

He picked up one of the soldiers.
"Even the general on horseback is
still here. It's been so long since I
have seen you," he said to the toy.
"You're coming along with me to
see if Maidy can get some of the
dirt off you!"

Prince Billy suddenly squealed with delight.

"I've always wanted a rocking horse and now I've got one!" he said excitedly. And, knocking off the bird's nest, he clambered up into the saddle and started rocking back and forth.

"The decorator must have accidentally papered over the door to the storeroom when we made the royal nursery for Rosie, and then it was forgotten about," said the Queen. "Well, now we can have great fun looking through it all!"

"We certainly did have an adventure," said Rosie to Ollie, who was busy rummaging around in a box containing bits of train set. "I'm rather glad you turned up today, Ollie! I'd never have found this secret playroom without you!"

And with that, she jumped onto
a big pile of dressing-up clothes
and quickly started to try on all
the hats she could find. "Yes, I think
I've finally found a real friend," she
said to herself. "What a brilliant
day this has been!"

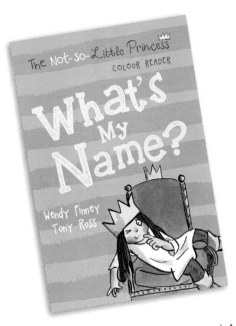

The Little Princess 👑

is not so little any more!

Now that she's growing up, people can't keep calling her the LITTLE Princess. But her real name is **horrible** and no one dares tell her what it is!

What will the Not-so-Little Princess do when she finds out?

Also available:

The Not-so-Little Princess:

What's My Name?
Where's Gilbert?
Spooky Night!

The Not-so-Little Princess
COLOUR READER

Best Friends!

Wendy Finney
Tony Ross

ANDERSEN PRESS

This edition published in 2017 by
Andersen Press Limited
20 Vauxhall Bridge Road
London SW1V 2SA
www.andersenpress.co.uk

First published in 2014 by
Andersen Press Limited

3 5 7 9 10 8 6 4 2

British Library Cataloguing in Publication Data available.

ISBN: 978 1 78344 511 0

Printed and bound in China